A Tale of
TWO Goats

Tom Barber
illustrated by Rosalind Beardshaw

To all of my mothers and fathers,
without whom I wouldn't have been possible
T.B.

For Kate, Paul and Loki
R. B. x

First published in Great Britain in 2005 by Gullane Children's Books
This paperback edition published in 2006 by

Gullane Children's Books
an imprint of Pinwheel Limited

Winchester House, 259-269 Old Marylebone Road,
London NW1 5XJ

1 3 5 7 9 10 8 6 4 2

Text © Tom Barber 2005
Illustrations © Rosalind Beardshaw 2005

The right of Tom Barber and Rosalind Beardshaw to be identified as the author and illustrator of this work
has been asserted by them in accordance with the Copyright, Designs and Patents Act, 1988.
A CIP record for this title is available from the British Library.

ISBN-13: 978-1-86233-608-7
ISBN-10: 1-86233-608-3

Printed and bound in China

A Tale of
TWO Goats

Tom Barber

illustrated by Rosalind Beardshaw

GULLANE
CHILDREN'S BOOKS

Farmer Cole lived all alone on a big farm in the middle of the prairie. His only companion was a goat called Myrtle. Every morning after milking he set her loose in a field of cabbages.

Next door was another big farm. Here lived Farmer Jones,
all on his own as well. His only friend was a goat called Muriel.
Every morning after milking he set her loose in a field of turnips.

Between Myrtle's field of cabbages and Muriel's field of turnips ran a fence of wood and wire. It had been started by Farmer Cole and added to by Farmer Jones. 'It's the only way to stop his greedy goat making off with my vegetables,' both farmers said to themselves.

Things may have stayed like this for ever,
had it not been for one awkward fact. Myrtle,
with her cabbages, preferred turnips and
Muriel, with her turnips, preferred cabbages.

Now, you must know that nothing can be allowed to come between a goat and its stomach. So Myrtle and Muriel had come up with a perfect solution to their problem. Every day, Myrtle pushed bits of cabbage through the wire to Muriel. Muriel, in turn, pushed bits of turnip through to Myrtle. This kept them both happy, and over the years they had become firm friends.

But then came the fateful day when Farmer Cole and
Farmer Jones finally noticed what the goats were up to.
'I can't have his goat chomping my cabbages,'
said Farmer Cole.
'I can't have his goat tucking into my turnips,'
said Farmer Jones.
'This must stop!' they both said.

So Farmer Cole
and Farmer
Jones collected
together wood
and nails.

Then they
set to,
hammering
and
sawing,
acting
for all the
world as
if the other
one simply
wasn't there.

They only stopped when there was not the tiniest
gap left where the goats might push through a morsel.

But goats' teeth are miraculously strong, and
the very next day Myrtle and Muriel gnawed a hole
right through the fence and carried on exactly as before.
Farmer Cole and Farmer Jones were on the look out for
trouble now. 'This won't do at all,' they muttered to themselves.

They brought bricks and mortar and in place of the fence, they built a wall. Even a goat can't chew through bricks!

But goats can dig when they have a mind.
So the very next day, Myrtle and Muriel tunnelled
right underneath the wall. They met up in the middle
and swapped turnip for cabbage as usual.

Well, the farmers weren't going to put up with that! They each dug a trench along their side of the wall and filled it in with concrete. *That will put a stop to this nonsense,* they thought.

And it did – for a while! But of course goats can throw pretty well. So Myrtle and Muriel tossed the turnips and cabbages over the wall to each other.

That took care of the food. But the truth was the two goats were missing the old days, when they could chat to each other, wattle to wattle, through the fence.

Meanwhile, Farmer Cole and Farmer Jones built the wall higher.

But goats, as you know,
are wicked climbers . . . !

So Farmer Cole and
Farmer Jones built the
wall even higher . . .

But goats can do a mean pole-vault – honest, I've seen them!

Farmer Cole and Farmer Jones had no choice but to build
the wall still higher. They topped it off with coils of wire.
'That should finish off their little game,' they
said to themselves. And, indeed, it did.

But now there was a new problem. Myrtle went right off her
food. All she could do was stare at the wall and bleat sadly.
From over the other side came a faint answering bleat,
for things were just as bad with Muriel.

Farmer Cole and Farmer Jones were worried. They tried everything – pea soup . . .

. . . best-peeled carrots, straw hats . . .

. . . even a turnip and a cabbage! But neither Myrtle or Muriel would take even a nibble.

Soon Myrtle and Muriel were nothing more than bags of bones. Farmer Cole and Farmer Jones were at their wits' end. As a last resort they called in the vet. He said the same to both of them. The farmers spent a restless night. In the morning they both carried their goats down to the field. Then they went back to fetch their tractors.

In ten minutes flat the wall was smashed to bits! Farmer Cole and Farmer Jones gazed at each other over the rubble. For the first time ever, instead of looking away, they gave each other a shy wave.

With the wall down, Myrtle and Muriel struggled to their feet. It was a touching reunion.

Myrtle was soon shredding a cabbage while Muriel got her teeth into a second turnip. Farmer Cole and Farmer Jones were so relieved to see their goats happy again. And with no fence there anymore it was hard to ignore each other. They were soon chatting away. It was amazing what they found to talk about – tractors, vegetables, milk – and goats!

Farmer Cole and Farmer Jones still
live on their own but they have their goats
and they have each other, and that seems
enough for all four of them . . .